Walt and Pepper

by Lisl Weil

Parents' Magazine Press / New York

LIBRARY OF CONGRESS CATALOGING IN PUBLICATION DATA
Weil, Lisl.
  Walt and Pepper.
  SUMMARY: A neighboring cat and dog think they are
enemies until one of them is missing for a while.
  [1. Cats—Fiction. 2. Dogs—Fiction] I. Title.
PZ7.W433Wal   [E]   73-22183
ISBN 0-8193-0758-0   ISBN 0-8193-0759-9 (lib. bdg.)

To my friends

Pizzi Tortissimo and Trash

Vicki, Beauregard and Cat,

Tutu and Mouse   Thomasina and Gertrude

Susie

and for Sepperl,
in memory

Walt lives across the street from Pepper.
Walt does not care for Pepper.

And Pepper does not care for Walt.
Not one bit.

"It's MY street," Walt thought, and he
bared his teeth so Pepper could see.

Pepper glared back at Walt. "It's MY street!"
And he showed *his* sharp nails.

"I'll chase you off my street," Walt growled,

"right up a tree so you can't get down,
you big blop."

"I'll chase YOU, you big good-for-nothing,

till you wished you were small enough to hide
in a mouse hole," Pepper hissed.

"Just you wait, I'll bite your ear off,"
Walt snapped, looking as mean as he could.

"Just watch yourself, I'll scratch you all over,"
Pepper hissed, making his fur stand on end.

Walt and Pepper certainly looked like enemies.

Every day they made mean faces at each other.

Every night each would dream
mean things about the other.

One day, Walt was not at his window.

He wasn't sitting there the next day either.

"The big good-for-nothing is hiding because he's afraid of me," Pepper thought to himself, very pleased.

The next week, the window across the street stayed empty.

Pepper strutted proudly back and forth on his windowsill.

At last the street was all his own!

Just the same, Pepper got up early every day
in case Walt did show up...

He really should be glad...

And feel happy...

and merry!

Yet, Pepper didn't.
He didn't enjoy his
favorite catnip anymore either.

"I don't know why Pepper looks so sad,"
the boy said.
"I don't know why Pepper is so listless,"
said his mother.

All day long Pepper dozed on his
windowsill. He didn't even glance at *his* street.

Nor did he notice when a taxicab stopped
below his windowsill.

People got out and lots of luggage was unloaded.

The next morning, Pepper dragged himself
up to his spot at the window. What else
was there to do but snooze away another day...

But who was waiting at the window across the way?
There was Walt, wagging his tail wildly!

"It's MY street," Walt growled over,
making a funny face.

"It's MY street," Pepper hissed back,
though it sounded more like a happy purr.

Now they were friends just playing a game.